Fannah

Flairs and Glairs
Publication House

Disclaimer

This is a work of fiction and solely represent the thoughts of the corresponding authors of the articles. Our editors have tried their best to edit the content of all the authors and check the plagiarism.

All the write-ups in this book are unique and are only published in this book.

In case any plagiarism or error is found, only the author is responsible alone, and not the publisher or the Compilers.

Cover Designing and Book Formatting

Shubham Shah and Ishani Agarwal

Acknowledgement

GOD-The Supreme, Thank you for blessing me with power and Zeal. Parents-The Guiding force, Thank you for trusting me and letting me work whenever I wanted.

When it comes to Anthology, My heartfelt thanks to Aishwarya Parida ma'am for helping me irrespective of her busy schedule. Thank you for working all night long and making this book a success. I will always be thankful to you for all kind of support, Guidance and Help. Compiling this book was one of my dream, it wouldn't have been completed without you. Thank you again.

I can't forget my 50 Co-Authors. Who always stood with me at my best and worst. Thank you from deepest core of my heart.

Much love to all of you

Co Author

Shubham Shah (Founder Flairs and Glairs)
Ishani Agarwal (Co-Founder Flairs and Glairs)
Faij Ahmad (Compiler)

1. Aishwarya Parida
2. Tusti Agarwal
3. Grishma Ninave
4. Ayushmam Majhi
5. Aryan Priyadarshi
6. Deepu Sharma
7. Krishnakant Singh
8. Anand Jain
9. Sahina Ghugha
10. Ayush Raj
11. Agam Sachdeva
12. Krishna Motwani
13. Bhavika Dhiraj Sindhi
14. Rashika Shaw
15. Priyanka Varma
16. Ankita Sahoo
17. Diksha Motwani
18. Tanya Gupta
19. Gunwanti Harish Thanvi
20. Dr. Sudhanya Nath
21. Urja Motwani
22. Roshan Khatun
23. Jude Fernandes

24. Gaurav Kumar
25. Ashish Santani
26. Zainab Saboowala
27. Rebecca Ann Oommen
28. Pramesh Kumar
29. Ms. Ishrat Jahan Noormohammed Khan
30. Rashmi Baweja
31. Kalamkaar
32. Srishty Singh
33. Sejal Soni
34. Adya Kumar
35. Ritu Kumari
36. Mohanapriya
37. Divyanshu Singh
38. Devendra Fagna
39. Payal Kamdi
40. Rahul Barman
41. Rupanjana Das
42. Sakshi Soni
43. Saurav Kumar
44. Supriti Vishwakarma
45. Shradha Gindlani
46. Ashiya Khatun
47. Ankita Nahar
48. Insha Nayyar
49. Rahul Kumar
50. Saddam Saikhaij Ahmad

Shubham Shah

(Founder- Flairs and Glairs)

Shubham Shah, an entrepreneur at "Flairs & Glairs" a brand with dynamics in events organizing and cultural educational pan INDIA, is a 26yrs old guy who recently has entered the digital platform of imprinting emotions. He has initiated with his own open mic platform to help budding poets and aspiring writers under his brand named as "Teekhe Zasbaaat"

He is a commerce graduate from the Bhagalpur City of Bihar.

He states Writing has impersonated him since childhood and he has now been writing for over a decade!

Cooking, on the other hand, is his passion! He also mentions, trying out new things just tickles him!

When asked sir, Why SPICY EMOTIONS?

He smiled and added, "agar jasbaat teekhe na ho toh wo jasbaat kahan" Spices are all that blends! So do his words!

As a chef, he presents to you his dish! Hot and freshly served! Taste it! Feel it! Enjoy it! You can also find his writing in the Book "Teekhe Zasbaaat" and 50+ Co-authored anthologies. With his passion to explore opportunities across Platforms, he is working with keen devotion and We wish him all the very best for his future ventures.

He is Featured in the International Magazine DeMode for his upcoming solo novel.

He is Approved by Ne8x for its Lit Fest, and is a Golden Star Awards 2020 Winner.

He is a India Book of Records Holder for his Anthology Satrang, and has the Grandmaster title by Asia Book of Records, for the same.

He has also been featured in Prabhat Khabar, Dainik Jagran, and a lot of other Newspapers in Bihar for his achievements.

He has been a proud co-author to

India Book Of Records (Title- Black)

World Book Of Records (Title -15 Wonders of Poetries)

India Book Of Records (Title - Aaina)

Vajra World Records Holder (Title - Gustakhi Maaf Hai)

High Range of Records Holder (Title - Gustakhi Maaf Hai)

Indian Book of Records

(Title - Road from Worst to Best)

Share your reviews on his

INSTAGRAM

> @spicy_emotions
> @shubham4shah

Or via email on

> shubham2shah@gmail.com

To stay tuned to his work and opportunities follow his business Handles

INSTAGRAM   FACEBOOK   YOUTUBE

> @flairsandglairs
> @teekhezasbaaat

WEBSITE:

> https://flairsandglairs.in/
> https://flairsandglairs.com/

Ishani Agarwal
(Co-Founder- Flairs and Glairs)

Ishani Agarwal hails from the City of Joy, Kolkata.

She is the co-founder of her Community "Teekhe Zasbaaat" and Flairs and Glairs Publication.

Been a Compiler for 45+ Anthologies, she is in the process for more. Co-authored in 150+ Anthologies. She is a India Book of Records Holder, a Vajra World Records Holder, a High Range of Records Holder, an OMG Book of Records Holder, a Bravo Record holder, a Forever Star Book of World Records and an Indian Book of Records Holder.

Approved by Ne8x for its Lit Fest 2020, and Literary Icon 2020. Also a Golden Star Awards Winner 2020.

She has also been awarded with India Star Republic Award 2021, a part of She Awards by Awards Arc and Winner of Nari Samman 2021 by Literoma.

She is also selected as Best Achiever of the Year by AwardsArc and Most Challenging Compiler Award by Spectrum Awards.
She got her first solo Published,a solo Compilation consisting of first 750 contents of hers, titled "Hand That Burnt While Healing".

She has been featured by the National Magazine "Taree Zameen Par" with the title 'unstoppable'.
Also featured in the International Magazine DeMode for her upcoming solo novel, she is proud to write on social issues, and is happy with the love she is receiving.
Connect with her on Instagram: @Ishani_agarwal_quotes / @compilations_so_far

Faij Ahmad

Faij Ahmad is a Free lance writer. He has Co-Authored 20+ Books and he has compiled 2 books so far. He writes on topic relating National Interest, Empowerment, Motivation and life at different spectra.

Currently he is Trainee Navigational officer cadet at shipping corporation of India under ministry of shipping, Govt of India.

A Proud Sainikian (Aryans, SS Gopalganj) 9th batch, Mavericks. He has done NCC for both the certificates "A" and "B". He has done Mountaineering Adventure Course from Nehru Institute of Mountaineering. He has also done Adventure course from National Adventure Institute, Panchmarhi. He is indian book of record holder and Asia book of record holder as well. Compiling this Book was his utmost need to synchronise his heart.

He is good at academics, Equally on ground. Hobbyist, he loves to play with the distance of celestial bodies (Moon and Stars).
Writing is not hobby, but his passion
He loves connecting People
You can catch him on Instagram
@shibbuahmed

My Heart Was Not Killed, It Was Murdered Infact

A sharp edge shining glass divided my heart into multiple parts. I was not broken but smashed with bow of feelings which tortured me for a month long. A happy face and shinning forehead was drowned intentionally by a coward force. Energy of togetherness escaped in dry air and I tasted a frozen insane flavour.

Hey,
I am okay and alright.
Celebrating happiness
Take my thankyou, adjust it somewhere in your ears and shut your vocals. Bow down your eyelids and keep your ears sharp on my words.

You had my heart but you hammered, tortured, squeezed, rubbed and kicked with zero kindness. You know what, I am obliged and humble enough for all unfair happenings. Because I am good and being good is crime.

Finnaly, I realised I am in a game with her, Gifting her winning stakes I left the platform. I left the platform.

Tujhe darr tha
Mai mukhalefat krunga teri
Magar, lanat hai tere ishq par

Takiya jo tha sirhane mere
Wo v bichhad gya
Ab kadmo unke, sar mera
Theek hu mai, mehfuz hu mai

Sard mausam aur khel-e-anzam tera
Bebak hu mai, paak hu mai
Na tu sahi, na khubsurat shakal teri
Has mat gusse ka gubbar hai ye

Khushkismat Tu
Likh rha soach kr tujhe
Na aziz, na abab, na asbab
Hai koi na kabil mere

Ganimat, unki izazat hai
Wrna dafan jis samandar me
Uske kabil bhi na tu
Has kr katra de dojak bhi
Iss kabil hai tu
Beta, iss kabil hai tu.

Aishwarya Parida

She is a girl of compassion and passion. Living with a moto of "Forward Ever". A Tilaiyan, Batch 11-18.
Writer by passion, singer by hobby. She loves to play with codes . She has strong interest in Back-End codes. Moreover she is into binary world. She is pursuing B-tech .

You can contact her on Instagram @devil.aish11

On the edge of piercing pin, I wear the nosepin of pride. Keeping my forehead on flame tip i mark my words "I was never wrong".

You destroyed my universe then with your cakes and hacks. On the basis of false assumptions you made me wrong. Okay, junk of my thrown sandel, Answer me today.
Did you win? , the snake dancing on your fallen forhead has forgotten the rythm. I am smiling with gear of importance and hell what, you snake tail. Bow down today, under my feat and feet. Because your are meant to behave same. Glad, you made your motion like this. Believe me, if "then" Would have been "now". I would have dredged you down after making sure your nose is smelling hell and tasting dirt. Bloody smuggler of silence, You have lost the potent to stand and create yourself. I'll not slap but punch on nostril tip to make you cry intentionally. Making you sit on back edge on sword, I will smile like devil.

My agreesion is touching hell and I am touching cloud. My spit will form rain and it will fall over your empty jerked brain. Your wrong story creation was having a big flaw In your flow database. I added yes in all tough times, I stood with all decision. But your standard was not enough to match mine. I have cleansed and polished all my shortcomings. Stalk and watch, snail of dimension less gutter.

My innocence asks, why another. When I used to nourish everything. Okay, your mental captivity has got zero kindness. But I have , leaving you below the shoe of my caretaker, my soulmaker. He will acknowledge all my pain and question you in the garden of truth. Your mouth will behave like open swollen flagpost. And he will fly the flag of courage and love, making you the Flag stand.
(Readers : situation was worse than my agreesion)

Tusti Agarwal

Tusti Agarwal is a content writer and a poet. Besides that she also loves to cook as she believes that 'The path of our heart passes through our stomach.'

Follow her on instagram @tusti_agarwal & @_feel_deep_

Hamne pyaar toh beshumaar kia unse,
Mano mohobbat ki jung thi, usse jeet lena tha mujhe

Apne dill ko unke hatho pe rakh dia ,
Hamme kya pta tha , unke hatho pe toh phool bhi nhi tikta .

Uss raahon par yuh nikli thi mai pyaar ka behkava le kar ,
Mano mohobbat ki dodd thi, usse bhi haasil kar lena tha
mujhe .

Uss pyaar ko pehechan dete dete kudh ki hi pehechan bhul si
gyi
Mano unse mohobbat karte karte khudse pyaar jatana hi bhul
gyi thi .

Khel rahe the vo mere dill se ,
agle hi lamhe,mera dill chutt gya unnke hatho se ,
Chutt kar bikhar gya yeh dill ,
Aur unke piaro ne rondh dala uss pyaar ko,
Mano mohobbat koi kaach ka khilona ho ...

Grishma Ninave

Grishma Ninave was born and brought up in the Orange City, Nagpur. She is a Science graduate and an avid reader. Thriller is her favourite genre. Currently working as a Project Head at Flairs & Glairs Publication House. Published in the Editorial section of a national magazine as Aaj Ki Womaniyaa, in the first edition of 2021. She won the Be The Change award 2021 organized by OMG book of records. A firm believer that happiness is not something that you find, it's something that you create. She loves travelling, blogging and listening to music.

You can follow her on insta @grish_ninave

The Hangover Of When I Last Met You

The hangover of when I last met you
still ponders over my head.
Where the eyes were grave
but still conveyed what they were not meant to...

The Hangover of when I last met you
is like a thunderstorm I wish to get rid of.
Where so less was spoken
but so much was said...

The hangover of when I last met you
Confuses me like a jigsaw puzzle.
Where the eyes seem to smile
and the lips seem to cry...

The hangover of when I last met you
is like the red sky.
Where the Sun loses its existence
only to give way to the moon....

क्यों आ गए हम इस मोड़ पर

क्यों आ गए हम इस मोड़ पर,
पिछले सारे रिश्तें तोड़ कर।

याद है आज भी जब तू पहली बार रोया था,
तुझे डर था कि तूने मुझे खोया था।

खुशी की लहर दौड़ जाती थी तेरी मुस्कान से,
पर आज भागती हूँ तेरी ही पहचान से।

इश्क़ होता तो रूठ जाती,
पर इबादत थी, ऐसे कैसे छूट जाती।

माना के साथी नहीं अब हम हैं,
पर दिल में आज भी तेरे न होने का ग़म है।

कोई आहट से लगता है कि तेरी परछाई है,
जो छुपके से मुझपे प्यार जताने आई है।

क्यों आ गए हम इस मोड़ पे,
पिछले सारे रिश्ते तोड़ के।

Ayushmaan Majhi

He is AYUSHMAN MAJHI from Odisha. An extremely talented and charming boy with immense excellence in the field of Music, Writing and Anchoring. He has received many awards in the field of Music, Writing and Anchoring.

Manly, manliness
A word used bit in jest
With distinct traits and quality
We are judged differently

He vomits anger
I spread love
He is reason of fight
I am conclusion of fight
He, A silence torturer
Me, A silence seeker

A soft man
Often greeted with snorts and giggles
People associate manliness with
Sitting in man caves
Drinking beer
Watching big game

But these are traits
Not the character, neither quality
People judge us differently
Whenever u mention manliness
Hope you use positively
It's has nothing to do with virtue

Aryan Priyadarshi

He is trainee navigational officer cadet at shipping corporation of India. Currently working for Axis bank. Addicted forever to a soul, Deep believer. A naval seafarer by profession and a writer by passion. He loves to mix compassion and enthusiasm in his work.

Memory never fades.

You can follow him on insta @munnaaryan3

Mai jata tha, dekhta tha, mehsoos karta tha us lamhe ko!!!
kyu...??

Kyu ki tum the us lamhe me.

Aaj v mai jata hu, dekhta hu, Lekin mehsoos nhi kar pata!!!
Kyu...??

Kyu ki tum nhi ho is lamhe me.

शुरू करते है फ़िर से मोहब्बत ।
तुम चले आओ।।

थोड़ा हम बदल जाते है।

थोड़ा तुम बदल जाओ।

Deepu Sharma

Happiness above everything. A man with strong potent, working as Assistant Manager in kissht.
You can follow him on insta @sharma.deepu_

ये छोड़ ना पुरानी बातें
आ चल नई कहानी बनाते हैं
बुरा तो सबका गया शाल
आ चल कुछ नया करते है
तू क्यों परेशान है इतना
आ चल मिलकर सुधारते हैं
खुश हो तू, मै हूं तेरे साथ
आ मिलकर साथ जीते हैं

Krishnakant Singh

Currently he is into C.Sc core. Love to play with codes and it's calibrations. He is deep into travelling and a photographer by passion. He loves distributing happiness, no matter what. You can follow him on insta @oopppss._

You know, what I feel
Sighting at crystal moon
Gazing at brown branches
In slow autumn
From my window

You know, what I feel
When I sit, Near the fire
Or on the body of log
Staring at impalpable ash

Bae, listen to me
Everything carries me to you
Aromas,lights, branches, ashes
Has got your face in them

Is it illusion or flashback
Whatever it is, but it pains
It's logical, but lame
I want to skip this game

I want to skip this game
I want to skip this game

Anand Jain

ANAND JAIN is a good writer from FAZILKA, PUNJAB
He has completed his GRADUATION in commerce stream.
From Panjab University.
He has been writing poetry for 3 years as his passion. With
the help of sister (sapna jain) and brother (Rakesh jain).
He wants to be a successful banker in future.
He is a founder of ROBIN HOOD ARMY, FAZILKA
(NGO).
You can follow him on insta @Anand_jain_12

करीब

आजा करीब इतने की इन साँसों को महका दे
बरसो से तरसती हुई इन बाँहों को सजा दे

इश्क की फरमाईश..ना रोक इन कदमों को,
तेरे जिस्म की खुशबू मेरी रूह में बसा दे

खेलूँ तेरी जुल्फों से.. .चुमू तेरे होठों को
कर प्यार आज इतना की मेरे होश उड़ा दे

मदहोश तेरी आँखें..कह रही हैं बहुत कुछ
आ पास मेरे इतना कि हर दूरी मिटा दे

ये गरम तेरी साँसें..टकराने दे मेरी साँसों से
शर्म ओ हया की तू आज दीवार गिरा दे

आजा करीब इतने की इन साँसों को मेहका दे.
बरसो से तरसती हुई इन बाँहों को सजा दे

ख्याल

मेरे ख्याल से तुम्हे भी मेरा ख्याल आता होगा,
क्या सोचता हूं तुम्हारे बारे में,
मन में ये सवाल तो आता होगा..

जैसे आ जाती है मुस्कुराहट मेरे चेहरे पे,
वैसे ही मेरा ज़िक्र भी तुम्हे हसा जाता होगा..

इंतज़ार रहता है जैसे मुझे तुझ से मिलने का,
वैसे ही मुझ से मिलने का ख्याल,
तुम्हे भी सताता होगा..

खोया रहता हूं मैं तुम्हारे ही ख्वाबों में जैसे,
वैसा कुछ ख्याल तुम्हारा भी,
रातों में हो जाता होगा..

बंद आंखो को तुम्हारी,
मेरा चेहरा नज़र आता होगा,
मेरे ख्याल से तुम्हे भी मेरा ख्याल आता होगा..

Sahina Ghugha

Sahina Ghugha is 20 year old b.com student at Saurashtra university Rajkot. She is from Jamnagar city of Gujarat. She is state level winner in poetry competition 2017. She is Co-author of 15+ anthologies. She is an amazing writer and poet and she wants do something for society through her pen.

Insta ID:- @ Itz_Sahina_write

छाला

तेरी तस्वीर ने बहते अश्क़ों को संभाला बहुत
तेरी तस्वीर के सहारे अश्क़ों को पाला बहुत

याद आता है रातों में तेरा वो दिल से खेलना
आज तक दिल के टुकड़ों को संभाला बहुत

ऐसा करो अब आ जाओ या साँसे छीन लो
निकल चुका अब अश्क़ों का दिवाला बहुत

नही देखी जाती मुझसे लाश अपने दिल की
निंगल चुके हैं हम तो ग़मों का निवाला बहुत

कौन हैं जो फोड़े मेरे दिल पर लगे छालों को
फ़ैल चुका है सीने पर धोखों का छाला बहुत

Ayush Raj

कागज़ की ये कश्ती मेरी , करना पार समंदर है
डूब न जाये मझधारों में , खौफ ये मन के अंदर है ..

A proud Mauryan
You can follow him on @_ayush.63_

फिर मिलेंगे चलते चलते

बड़े सुकून मिलते थे , आपकी हेल्लो - हाय से
और ज़ख्म भी गहरे निकले , Take care ! Goodbye से
बेवकूफ दिल था मेरा , जो आपकी इबादत किया करता था
अरे वो तो तस्वीरों से भी बेइंतहां , मोहब्बत किया करता था ।

कभी याद मेरी आये तो , हँस के भुला दीजियेगा
अगर रोना ही हो , तो पहले हमें रुला दीजियेगा
इसके बाद भी खुदा की आप पर उतनी ही इनायत हो
यहीं दुआ है मेरी कि , ज़िन्दगी आपकी सलामत हो

सीख लीजियेगा जीना हँसते - हँसते
कहना था यहीं जाते - जाते
हमारा क्या .. हम हैं राही प्यार के
फिर मिलेंगे चलते चलते ।

Agam Sachdeva

She is an extremely talented girl with a very beautiful mind. She writes so well at such a young age. Though, she is just 14 years old but still is adored by many people. She has been a part of many anthologies earlier and has made her parents proud. She is a beautiful creation of God.
You can follow her on @_storyteller_agam_

A Fake Promise

Promise is a strong word. Please don't take it for granted. It's supposed to be cherished. And some use to to make our fool. If you have promised. Give your best to keep it. Because when a promise is broken. Our heart rips away. It is betrayed, I don't know who should I blame. But my heart bleeds. And my tears dried up. Now, the thing will never be the same. It is ripped away already. A Fake Promise was made. And couldn't be fixed with any first aid. You broke our promise, just because your friend now again. Wants to get back with you. Don't you remember I stood with you. When he ripped your heart away? Now, I found out, and I gave a silent but very loud scream. I have learnt a lesson this way. That these are just your bad days. You broke me completely, my promise was broken, my trust scattered like you again, broke, a glass in the kitchen, you hurt me still I couldn't stop loving you. Dammit! You even took my love. For granted, And faked, But, you better remember, you didn't just faked me. But yourself too, future has your result ready, you better be ready to pay, for your bad say.

Trust

It hurts so badly
When I think of what you have done
I want to leave you behind
But I don't have courage to run
I don't want to break anyone's trust,
Who's I actually won
It will not benefit me and not make me earn!

Once trust is broken
It's very difficult to fix it
All the new promises you make to me
Will never fit
Our story will not reach 100 and century
Will be hit
Instead, it will be buried into a pit
Our love will get as small as eyelens kit
And we will break our every bit.

Krishn Motwani

Krishna Motwani is a Student currently.
She use to pen down her feelings.
She is a moody girl. She started writing in the month of june,2020. She writes in her free time. She writes some motivational quotes or poetries too and practices artworks also.She lives her life like a bird
As bird flies freely and enjoys life like that she also lives her life freely and enjoy fullest.For motivating and inspiring poems and quotes, you can check her on instagram : @ unique__blog_

Move Ahead Now!

She was little bit confused,
But she never refused.

Her life was too tough,
Her life that person whom she loved but he did bluff.

She was in tough situation,
She controlled all, like her heart was a creation.

She forgot all his bad days now,
Now her smile comes with a new glow.

She use to forgot all the things happened in past,
She thinks that days Spended with him were last.

Now she inspire heart,
To go apart.

She knows that she will go ahead,
She tied her heart with a thread.

She will do with happiness,
And forgot all sadness!

Bhavika Dhiraj Sindhi

Bhavika Dhiraj Sindhi a 25 year old creative writer. She belongs to Turkey an Indian writing from abroad due to her passion in writing..A bcom graduate..She uses her pen as a best friend to speak her feelings.
 You can follow her on @she_is_troublesome

Doors That Shut Apart...

She had a miscarriage...
All the years of marriage when she was low he made sure to support...
And the other way round when he was down she was the one who got him bloom...
Since that day both were broken...
Felt betrayed...
It was neither one's fault...
Drowned and broken left apart...
Her trauma killed her all inside...
She was home with all dead inside...
He was all broken...
But the expectation they both had was no more a part of life...
Each day seeing each other just going with their chores...
None made up each other's mood...
Both struggling inside to pass each day hard..
Each one started blaming each other for the thing that had happened...
He started drinking and harassing her...
 She busted in tears and anger she started cursing herself and hurted her..
It was just a phase that needed patience love and care and
Thy,shall have a happy family back
The ones who used to be lovebirds...
Didn't wish to see each other's face...
All they played was a blame game...
Which got them to different paths...
The slammed doors the harsh words
Stay made it worst...
Finally they decided to stay apart...
Because love didn't win over anger...

To the worst days of life when they needed each other..
All they did was teared each other...
Hence none came forward little words that broke the hearts apart...
All the promises of forever together were broken...
Both felt lost and hurted...
To the love who wished the same from the shooting star asking for infinity love...
Forgot all...
The God conveyed...
To the one lost life who made them apart was in the hands of god..
She just came to test their love...
God wanted to see their true love..
If they would be a strong wall for each other they would have been blessed with the twins...
That was the blessing if they would stay instead of betraying each other...

Rashika Shaw

Professional writer, passionate about dancing, traveling and exploring new things and places...
You can follow her on insta @alfaaz_e_rashika

भूलना मुश्किल है तूझे, पर
भूलना होगा मूझे...
राहों पर इश्क की लाया
तूने ही था मूझे...
अब मजधार में छोड़ कर
जा रहा है तू मूझे...
बिन तेरे रहना सिखना
होगा मूझे...
भूलना मुश्किल है तूझे,
 पर भूलना होगा मूझे...

आसान है कया...
किसी को पाकर यूँ खो देना,
रूह का जिस्म से यूँ जुदा होना,
आसान है कया...
तेरी बातों, तेरी यादों को यूँ भूलाना,
तेरे संग बिताए वो पल,
ज़हन से यूँ निकालना,
आसान है कया...
हाँ सुनने में तो बहुत ही
आसान लगता है...
मगर धड़कन को दिल से यूँ जुदा
करना आसान है कया...

Priyanka Varma

She is Priyanka Varma studying Master's of Pharmacy from Visakhapatnam. She is a National and Central Zonal Sports Player along with being a Classical Dancer and an Artist. Along with these, She is also a poetess fond of writing her thoughts.

You can follow her on insta @priyanka_varma_

My Wrist

Red as the blood gushing from my wrist.
My body aches for love,
I Promised myself
I wouldn't let you
Become just words on a page
Guess that this means
You went and broke my heart
Ignoring me, is that how you treat everyone?
I slit my wrists
You watch me bleed
I slit my wrists for you to see
How much pain you've given me
And how much you really mean to me
I slit my wrists
I watch myself bleed
I slit my wrists tears pouring down my cheeks
I'm getting weak
I fall to the ground to fall asleep
Never to wake up again
Just don't come back with the purpose of twisting the wrist
of my feelings

Ankita Sahoo

She is a student and is currently doing her graduation in political science. She is a bibliophile and an extremely passionate writer. She is a co-author in many anthologies and is willing to work more . She wants to be an IAS officer and serve the nation.

You can follow her on @ankitasahoo__

It's still in my mind how you left me,
All alone behind and went away,
I agree you exactly didn't ,
But the reason why I moved away from you was you only,
You promised not to betray me,
But you did,you were with someone else when I needed you the most,
I haven't approached you,
You did that and you only left,
That incident still gives me a crack in heart,
It would never leave me,
It keeps snatching me in my dreams,
My feelings,emotions were all broken,
A heart break which was left unsaid,
I moved away from you just for you,
Thinking you would be happy without me,
But then you realised my love,
You wanted to come back,
Asked me for another chance,
Facing lots of difficulties now that we are together,
Don't break my heart,
Just be with me forever and ever.

Diksha Motwani

Diksha Motwani   is a passionate girl from Mumbai, Maharashtra. She loves to pen her feelings. She is introvert but her pen makes her extrovert. She is a writer, singer, artist and a poet!
Ig: @radha_1229

Love Art !

Groaning on my bed,
Old chats I read,
Loved you alot,
Cried for you alot,
You left me with broken heart,
All of it was your fake love art.

Tanya Gupta

Tanya Gupta is a student at Department of Zoology, Panjab University, Chandigarh and currently pursuing M.Sc.(Hons.) Zoology. Her academic passion is life sciences and together with this, she is passionate for creative writing especially poems. She has written many pieces in different genres and successfully participated in different poetic events. She is a practitioner of Heartfulnness meditation.

पता है जब किसी और के लिए तू गया था मुझे छोड़,
दिया था तब तूने मेरा दिल तोड़।
तेरी तस्वीर देखकर ही होती थी मेरे दिन कि शुरुआत,
और तुझे देखकर ही हसीन बनती थी मेरी हर रात।
मगर अब बहुत दिन हो गये तेरी तस्वीर नहीं देखी।
मैं खुश होती थी तो लगता था बस झट से तुझे अपनी खुशी बतादूँ,
दुखी होती तो बस लगता की तुझे रोकर अपना गम सुनादूँ ।
पर अब तू है नहीं तो सब खुद से साँझा करती हूँ।
वो हर लम्हा तुझसे जुडा सामने था आता,
छुपाने की कोशिश करती पर यह दर्द ना चुप पाता।
लेकिन अब तू नहीं बस मैं हूँ सिर्फ मैं।
हाँ तेरी याद तो बहुत आती थी,
धोका दिया तूने मुझे,
मगर अब खुद से प्यार करना मैंने सीख लिया।
खुद के साथ ही खुश रहना मैंने सीख लिया।

Gunwanti Harish Thanvi

Gunwanti Harish Thanvi (Sonu)
A girl with lot of dreams, and a passion to prove herself, Still a student, trying to make her dreams true. Born in Rajasthan. Science student, an upcoming writer. She likes to write what she feels, and loves to do what she wants to rather than thinking about the world's saying. She is a friend who is always to help people when they need her, even they are her enemies. She loves to listen music, and has very less friends. Her world is her mom and she loves her the most. You can follow her on insta @Strings_of_heart7

Galti

Aisi bhi kya galti kar di humne,
Jo hame chhod kar chal diye,
Naraazgi kya itni achi hai humse,
Naa jaane kitna dur chal diye humse,
Chhodna hi tha toh pehle aaye hi kyu the,
Aur aaye the toh jane ki kya jarurat padh gai....

Yaad

Ek taraf teri choti choti baatein yaad aati hai,
Aur dursi dafa tumhari vo choti si muskurahat yaad aati hai,
Bin bataya tumhare yu chale aana yaad aata hai,
Aur bin kuch kahe meri fikar karna yaad aata hai,
Tumhari dil ki har dehleez par humara likha naam yaad aata hai,
Yeh ab sapne jaise hai lagte hai,
Bas tumhare hame yu chhod kar chale jaana yaad aata hai....

Dr. Sudhanya Nath

A veterinarian, pursuing her PhD degree from WBUAFS,Kolkata. She was conferred InSc Young Achiever Award, Vajra World Records, International Research Awards on New Science Inventions,Inspiring Lady Veterinarian Award 2021.She has contributed in 50+ Antho.She is Founder of World of Logophiles, English Judge and Challenge Head of Peaceful Writers International and Community Head of Author Revolution. On OCT 4 2020, she was recognized by TOI and local newspaper Dharitri for making the best use of lockdown by achieving 325 E-certificates.

Perfidious Love

You shattered all of my hopes and dreams,
You changed the meaning of love,
I feel so helpless from my heart,
That I am left with no energy to scream.

I don't know what to do now,
I don't understand what went wrong,
I can't realize why this happened and how,
I can't accept the fact that you alienated me for someone else.

The magical feeling which I once had for you,
Is gone now taking all those lovely vibes.
I don't know whether,
I can again love and trust someone or not.

You have completely broken me,
My heart is throbbing,
And I wish it to be just a nightmare,
But every morning I have to console myself to face the
reality.

I am trying to gather all those broken pieces,
Which my eyes saw falling apart,
I know sooner or later I will overcome this pain,
And life will bless me with all the things which I deserve.

Urja Motwani

Urja Motwani a 21 year old writer she has completed her bmm recently. She is fashion and travel enthusiast and loves to write her feelings

You can follow her on insta @Motwani_urja

Love To Betrayals

My first love
The man i feel in head over heels
He decided to have a relationship he was not sure about
He spoiled the meaning of love for it was not easy getting
over him he was my best friend it was like i lost both
because he was not sure about his feelings
Then why would you lie to me why would someone propose
to me in front of 20 people if you were not sure about me if
you really didn't feel you could have talked to me about your
feelings that you have mixed feelings
You were my first person always no matter what you could
share your happiness but you couldn't share you thought with
me you promised me stars the happiness the world you told
me i was your family you so i always trusted you no matter
how bad your days were because i knew the importance of
being there holding hands how up or low our lives are you
had your space your freedom as well i had but you betrayed
that trust when you started to do the smallest thing like
giving me less minutes because you were talking to her &
when you started to forget to bring me chocolates later when
i came to know the chocolates were going to her instead it
hurtss yess i may sound cliche i don't care it was never about
the chocolates it was about your love for me it was my
favorite moment of the day having chocolate with you. I was
shattered when i saw you the way you looked at her she knew
i was your girlfriend but it didn't seem like because she was
more important to you then i was you didn't remember me all
you could see was her i was like the side support friend you
didn't misused me you were a gentleman but you you used
my blind trust ,you took the liberty to break my heart in a
way i can't imagine you ruined our friendship you betrayed
my love when you were not sure about yours

Roshan Khatun

Roshan Khatun, a person who is busy to finding peace because peace is the world's most precious thing.

You can follow her on insta @Iroshnikhatun

Malang ho kar tujhe me fannah mai ho jawa,
Dil ki jameen me ghum teri chah mai ho jawa.

Zidd me teri mai tamanah ban ubharte jawa,
Hasil kar is junnon ko har mumkin jaha mai ho jawa.

Asar hai qatil tera mujhe jaise huyi mai malang,
Ban kar teri inayat teri raah mai ho jawa.

Bewafa lage jo yeh jahan tujhe wafa ka sabar,
Dekh kar tu mujhe jaise nigah mai ho jawa.

Karke hasil ho tujhe woh ho jaw mai shaza,
Karke sukun mile jo tujhe woh gunnah mai ho jawa.

Teri jaan par bat aaye toh tujhe sawar kar,
'Roshan' De ke daga khud tabah mai ho jawa.

Teri Yaad Na aaye aisa ek din nahi gaya,
Tu mera nahi phir tere liye meri ishq kabhi kam nahi gaya.

Jude Fernandes

Currently pursuing a Masters in English Degree from Goa University - Taleigao, Jude is an enthusiastic student residing in Vasco da Gama, Goa - India.

His passionate talents in literature, creative writing, music, acting, sketching and public speaking have secured numerous awards at school, college and State levels. He is also a published co-author of 60+ national and international anthologies.

Instagram Handle: @jude_fernandes_official

Betrayed

You promised the world:
a magical wonderland;
you and I, sparkling diamonds,
carving destiny together!

You promised happily-ever-afters:
a spectacular wedding;
you and I, spendthrift lives,
though I never demanded it.

You promised satisfaction:
a union never to be fractured;
you and I, always rejoicing,
no room for bitterness or revenge.

You promised it all, repeatedly:
and I, naïve heart, fell for it.
Regret is frustrating,
but I sure have learned some lessons.

Gaurav Kumar

Passionate about football and writting,he is an established poet and writer.He has previously been part of renowned anthology "SAINIK'S INKED BLOOD" by FLAIRS AND GLAIRS.

You can follow him on insta @Gauravvats_2

रिश्ते

सोचा था तुझ संग ज़िन्दगी गुज़ारने का,
पर तुझे तो मुझसे पल्ला झाड़ना था,
जोड़े थे तुझ संग नाते सारे,
पर तुझे तो मुझसे रिश्ता बिगाड़ना था,

तू चाहती तो मेरी गलतियों को माफ़ कर सकती थी,
पर उन्हें याद दिला कर तुझे मुझको लताड़ना था,
शायद मैं उतना सुन्दर और साफ़ न था,
तभी तो तुझे मुझसे रिश्ता बिगाड़ना था,

रिश्ता टूटने की वजह धोखेबाज़ी हो तो ग़म नहीं,
पर यहाँ तो गलतफहमियों का झरना था,
शायद मेरे लिए तेरी अच्छी सोच हालत सुधर सकती थी,
पर तुझे तो मुझसे पल्ला झाड़ना था,

तेरे साथ बिताया हुआ हर एक पल कांटे की तरह चुभता है,
क्यों किया मैंने कुछ भी, मेरा ज़हन बार बार पूछता है,
गलत समझ बैठी तू मेरे प्यार को,
शायद तुझे मुझको उन बातों को लेकर लताड़ना था,

हमेशा की तरह तू जीत गयी और मैं हार गया,
शायद हमारे नसीब में सिर्फ झगड़ना था,
प्यार न हो सका तुझे मुझसे,
शायद हमेशा ही तुझे मुझसे पल्ला झड़ना था,
तभी तो तुझे मुझसे रिश्ता बिगाड़ना था....

Ashish Santani

Professionally a Musician, Vocalist and Music Teacher In Art Anima Academy Of Music, Raipur, Chhattisgarh, Ashish Santani is an occasional hindi writer. He writes poetries for self Motivation and is a lyrics Writer as per swings. Additionally he has been a co-authors of multiple anthologies and is continuing in the same. Follow him in his Instagram handle @enterrocker

"हम फ़िर मिलेंगे"

सारे जहां के दर्द बेज़ार हो जाते
जब तेरे नैनों के दीदार हो जाते
अब बस तेरी यादों कि लौ ही दिखती है
और ये आंखें मोम सी पिघलती है

अब ना तू है साथ ना तन्हाई है
जागू या सोऊ तेरे ख्वाबों की परछाईं है
बस ठैहैर जा मेरी रूह के मस्तक में
ताकि दे सकू तेरी रूह को तस्तक में

ये नसीब ये किस्मत
सब बेबस ही रहेंगे
बस तू एक इशारा कर दे
हम तेरे ही होके रहेंगे
ये चांद ये तारे
सब साथ ही चलेंगे
तेरा इंतजार रहेगा

क्योंकि हम फ़िर मिलेंगे।

Zainab Saboowala

Zainab Saboowala is a dreamer and believer from Mumbai. She's a night lover and works on being a good human rather than great one. Her writings are her thoughts, emotions and feelings put into words. She believes when you can't say it, write it. She is optimistic and loves spreading smiles around.

Pen name - Zain ;
Instagram handle - @an.affectionate.dreamer

Broken Ties

We were good friends before you asked me out
I knew you loved me in a way no friend does
Jealousy you tried to hide use to be so evident
Every little thing you did to make me smile
All those sweet gestures that made me feel so special
You said you saw the beautiful me which I couldn't see
You said you wish that one day I could be yours
You convinced me to give love a chance, no matter even if
we drift apart
Nothing would ever change
The friendship we have will always stay
I believed every word you said to me
I believed all those gestures were true
It wasn't love I believed in
But I believed in you
I gave my trust, myself to you
All you did was crush it like a trash
And then expected from me to be just friend
I knew love would hurt,
But I put my trust on you and that hurts more
I had a friend before I found love in you
Now I've lost the belief that love can ever be true
And I've lost my friend too.

Rebecca Ann Oommen

She is just a 15 year old girl who has seen enough in life to know how to live it. She wants her work to be a knowledge by others and if possible give them support through her work. You can follow her on insta @__.rebeccaa.___

Maybe We Weren't

Maybe we weren't meant to be together
Maybe We weren't meant to live forever.
Our legs weren't meant to stay mingled together
Our hands weren't meant to be tangled forever.
Maybe our happy moments were meant to turn into painful memories
Our deep conversations are now just meaningless stories.
Maybe you weren't mine to keep
Maybe All these things were the reasons why we weren't meant to be.

Broken Promises

Maybe we were the definition of right person wrong time. I wish when we both meet in our next lives again, Let's fall in love all over again. But this time without regrets, without pain, without misunderstandings and most importantly without broken promises.

Pramesh Kumar

Pramesh Kumar, a writer who writes from his innermost. He is very clear and subtle in his writing and a person who pours down an ocean of thought in a flow of just a few words. His minute observation of worldly things and aspects gives a charm in his writing. After all he is a lover of nature and humanity. He rightly says about his writing, "Every word of my writing is not only a combination of letters but my heartbeat which gives life to my literary arts".You can follow him on insta @primewriter007

फासले तेरे मेरे दरमियां

तुमसे वो पहली मुलाकात आख़िरी होती तो अच्छा था
दिल में उतर जाने वाली वो बातें आख़िरी होती तो अच्छा था
काश जुड़ने से पहले जुदा हो गए होते रास्ते हमारे
और मोहब्बत की वो बातें आख़िरी होती तो अच्छा था।

"अब भला क्या चाहूँगा मैं इस नाकामयाब मोहब्बत से"
अब तो नफ़रत उगलने वाली ये बातें आख़िरी हों तो अच्छा था
जो भी शिकायत है तुम्हें मुझसे, मैं दिल से क़ुबूल करता हूँ
बस ये हर बार चुभने वाली बातें आख़िरी हों तो अच्छा था।

गर..बाकी हों कुछ दर्द ,तो दे दो, गर दिल चाहे तुम्हारा
अब तमन्ना बस... के ये रिश्ता आख़िरी हो तो अच्छा था।

Ms. Ishrat Jahan Noormohammed Khan

Ms Ishrat jahan khan is a passionate Teacher and a Writer she loves reading and writing. Loving and caring is her hobby. And keep learning and accept the positive suggestion is her quality.

She belongs to North India and stays at Ulhasnagar (Maharashtra).

Loves humanity always.

You can follow her on insta @ishrat7755

फनाह

एक छोटी सी गुन्हा हो जाये
किसी हमदर्द पे दिल फनाह हो जाये

जिंदगी चलती रहे
और हम भी चलते रहे

धीरे धीरे जिंदगी में
कमी ना आये हर खुशी में

लड़ाई भी हो जरूरी
बाते करना भी हो मजबूरी

कभी हो ना दूरी
कोई हो ना कमजोरी

दिल धड़के दोनों का
हर पल हो मन मिलने का

ऐसे जिंदगी ना तन्हा हो जाये
बस किसी अपने पे फनहा हो जाये

Quotes

1.Love to be share
Only there should be care
No one should dare
Love is to be share

2.Happy to be with
Love with twist
Feeling of loneliness
With always friendliness

3.To give is easy
But the person is always busy
You make a hope
Which further can't cope...

Rashmi Baweja

रश्मी इस कहानी की लेखिका बिल्कुल अपने नाम के अनुरूप ही सबके जीवन को प्रकाशित करती है। रश्मी हरियाणा के सोनीपत जिले की निवासी है। उन्होंने MCA किया है। उन्होंने अपना लेखन कार्य 2016 में प्रारंभ किया।वे फेसबुक पर HEART TOUCHING पेज पर भी लिखती हैंlhttps://www.facebook.com/rashmibaweja1993/अलग अलग विषयों पर वे बहुत अच्छा लिखती हैं।अपने अनुभवों व दूसरों को समझने के अपने हुनर के आधार पर ही वे अपनी रचना लेकर आई हैं।

जाते जाते वो मुझे ज़िन्दगी के दो सबक दे गया था।
धोखे के साथ ज़िन्दगी जीने की नई वजह दे गया था।
आज जिस मौक़ाम पर हूँ शायद कभी हासिल नही कर पाती।
इसलिए सोचती हूँ ज़िन्दगी में आगे बढ़ने के लिए धोखा भी जरूरी
था।।

मुझे जाते जाते भी वो साहस से भरी चुनोतियाँ दे गया था।
ज़िन्दगी में कुछ नही कर सकती मैं कभी ये उपहास उड़ा गया था।
उसके जाने को मैंने कमजोरी नही अपनी ताकत बना लिया।
इसलिए सोचती हूँ ज़िन्दगी में आगे बढ़ने के लिए धोखा भी जरूरी
था।।

धोखे के बाद ज़िन्दगी में खुद को टूटने नही दिया था
दो सफर में ज़िन्दगी में आगे बढ़ने का सफर चुन लिया था।
माना याद आती है मुझे अब तक उसकी बहुत पर खुद को पक्का
कर लिया था।
इसलिए सोचती हूँ ज़िन्दगी में आगे बढ़ने के लिए धोखा भी जरूरी
था।।

जाते जाते वो मेरी नाकामयाबी को छोड़ने की वजह बता गया था।
मेरे मन मे जैसे आग से भड़का हुआ एक जुनून जगा गया था।
आज ज़िन्दगी में एक लेखक बन कर सच्चा सुकून मुझे मिला है।
इसलिए सोचती हूँ ज़िन्दगी में आगे बढ़ने के लिए धोखा भी जरूरी
था।।

Kalamkaar

This is Kalamkaar. He is from Uttrakhand bought up in Meerut(Up). His hobbies are reading and writing. His interest is in writing. He love writing. He is part of440+Anthologies as Co-Author. He won 500+ Certificate in Writing, He Start writing 29 February 2020. He is part of 7 anthology as Co Author going for record and He is omg record holder as Co - Author of Book Called Laposia. He is simple and people observer. His insta handle is kalamkaar51 and e-mail kalamkaar51@gmail.com. He believes in Karma.

आखरी उम्मीद

छोड़ गयी तन्हा मुझे अकेले जिंदगी की राह मे,
रोका नहीं किसी ने यार दोस्त भी थे मेरे साथ मे ।
हार गया इश्क़ की लड़ाई मे ना होगा कोई भी मीत ,
क्योकि वो ही थी मेरे जीने की आखरी उम्मीद ।
भूल गयी वो सारे कसमें वादे
ना जाने कैसे बदल गये उसके इरादे ,
छोड़ने से पहले अगर हुई हो गलती वो बता दे ।
मिल गयी अगर तो जिंदगी की दौड़ मे हार के भी जाऊँगा जीत ,
क्योकि मेरे डगमगाते कदमों को सँभालने वाली वही थी आखरी
उम्मीद।
अब कैसे गुजारूँगा जिंदगी उसके बगैर
जो ले गया दूर उसको मुझसे उसकी नहीं खैर
अब उसका हैं सीधा मुझसे बैर ,
याद करता हूँ उन लम्हों को जब जाते थे हम करने सैर ।
जो संभाल सकता हैं मुझे बुरी आदतों से और भर दे मेरी बेसुरी
जिंदगी मे सुरीले गीत ,
वही हैं एक आखरी उम्मीद ।
जो मेरे टूटे हुए दिल को जोड़ सके,
मुझसे दूर जाते रास्ते उसके मुझ तक मोड़ सके ।
बुरी आदतों मे जाने से जो मुझे रोक सके ,
जो मेरा बुरा करना चाहें उनके मंसूबो को रोक सके ।
सफलता पाने के लिए मुझे प्रेरित करने के लिए ख़ुद को झोंक सके।
जो मेरी जिंदगी की विश्वास की पोटली को भर सके ,
जो खुदसे ज्यादा मुझ पर भरोसा रख सके ।
मेरे लिए जो बुरे वक़्त मे हौसला रख सके ,
जो तोड़े मेरी असफल होने की रीत
वही हैं मेरी आखरी उम्मीद ।

Srishty Singh

This Is Srishty Singh, A Passionate Writer From Jharkhand. She Has Contributed To 100+ Anthologies As A Co-Author. She Is A Project Head Under Fortify Teen And Flaming Pens Publication, Head Task Operator Under Inner Souls Community, Manager Under Inkzoid Foundation And Fortify Teen, Challenge Head Under Team Writers, Community Head Under World Of Logophiles Community And Graphic Head Under Sunshine Publication.
You Can Follow Her On Insta @Srishty_28_Singh

Dear Destroyer

Dear destroyer,
Just found a little black cranny
In the corner of my heart
Dull, tedious but yet excruciating.
I realized it's you, the same you,
Domineer, insolent, dubious
But no more deleterious
Just a silent, dead spot.
Why are you still there,
To inflict the pain again
From the lover to the ravager
Why don't you leave my heart?
If you still wanna come back,
Come with all your phantasm
'Cause this time I'm ready
For all your betrayal and treachery.
'Cause this time I won't destroy
I'll leave for my peace, my death.

Sejal Soni

I am as simple as quantum physics. A big home of fortune lies inside me. Destined to achieve zenith, Sorted to win.

You can follow her on insta @Sejalsoni1016

Anchoring in harbour
We're standing little boats
Middling, they sails
In screaming wind
They shiver
When thunder claps
They are blind
When it rains
But in this night
I shall row

Beautifully lined up
In order they move
The skipper is ready
Waiting for the command
But, hold on
Let sun sets down
And move on
When its dark salty water

Just because
I don't fear, if it's dark
I don't stuck, when waves are cruel
Don't have fear of night
I rule in darkest of sight
I am king of my own night
I am king of my own night

Adya Kumar

Adya is a student of class 11 and writing for her is like a refreshing cup of coffee and it makes her feel lively. Pouring her heart out onto the paper makes her feel light.

You can follow him on insta @illusionary.tranquility

Respect

I will never say that you didn't love me
I will never say that you weren't there for me
I will never say you didn't care for me
But i will always say you didn't respect me
You didn't respect my love for you
You didn't respect my affection towards you
So i will not hold on to the hope that you will comeback
Because you hurt me.

Dear Ex,

I loved you more than my words every expressed, i held you more firmly than you ever felt and i cared for you more than i ever said but you know as i walk away from you today i no longer feel the pain it is a vast emptiness and i no longer feel the need to keep you close because maybe you hurt me more that i ever expressed, maybe you pushed me more than i ever felt and maybe you made me cry more than i ever said.

Ritu Kumari

Ritu kumari, Feat hunny. She is girl with high understanding and liable enough to be good friend of everyone. She is master of her mind and queen of her heart. She is in search of peace with heavy heart. Decent, strong and a girl with high potent.

Aaina bhi chamak utha
Shakal meri dekh ke
Us din tuta tha mai

Sun rakib, zara hiqmat kr
Meri hasrat sun

Ho na ski apni mohabbat muqammal
Sayad manjur-e-khuda na tha

Zalim duniya, zulm hazar
Neki ke tarazu pe apni ishq sawar

Sun habib, chhod ishq
Aa zara dosti kr le

Naseeb hi aisi ya khel-e-taqdeer hai
Jo bhi hai, ab sb manjur hai

Tera haath ni, ab bs saath chahiye
Hu waqif tere rag se
Ab pokhta imaan chahiye
Mehej dosti
Lekin tere jaisa insaan chahiye
Lekin tere jaisa insaan chahiye

Mohanapriya.K

Co-author Mohanapriya.K is a good writer from Tamilnadu, India. She has completed her Bachelor's degree in Engineering stream. She has been a writer for one year as her passion. She wants to be a best compiler and curator in future. She is very happy to undertake such noble art. Yet she sincerely hope that this writing journey of her will continue as sweetly as it is now and will bring her many successes. She also loves singing, gardening and drawing.

I.G : @colours_honey_official

E-mail : doraa.kutty@gmail.com

He Was The One Who Betrayed Me That True Love Also Fails

Only memories of you make me very strong. At the same time they are the only ones that make me so weak. I know you will never come back to me. Even so, your memories alone are something that refuses to leave me? There is nothing more cruel in this world than breakup. I thought my love would be with me until the last, and I longed to be. But now my love is not with me and has left me. My top love for him and my top love for him. But he has more love for money than me. That's why he went in search of a woman richer than me. It's been a year since we first met. He is more interested in taking photos. My desire is to take more photos of myself too. He has fulfilled this desire of mine many times and has rejected it. I bought a camera for him and gifted it to him. It was a very lucky camera because I was not allowed to be with him but that camera is still with him today. Because that camera has become costly. He didn't even think about how hard I worked to buy that camera for him. But for that I am not angry at all because the love I have for him is so real. He should be happy today.

The Mistakes I Make Also Make Me Realize That There Is No Life Without Mistakes

There can be no man in this world without making mistakes. In other words, mistakes make a man. mistakes But it is our duty to correct the mistake we have made without repeating it. It is our duty to correct that! What one person may have experienced may not have been experienced by another. It all depends on the way he lives and his qualities. So do not try to control others with your experience. All living beings in this world go in search of pleasures. So we need to make decisions even when we know the circumstances around us. Teach them to live life as it is, to live it as it is, but not to put order and rules as it should be. We really think we should hate some people in our lives but we can never completely hate them for what we think we are. We do not know when or what will happen in our life, the next minute is a life of uncertainty, so learn to live the life you live in peace and happiness. Your self confidence and inner trust on you give you wings. Just accept yourself, fly high what distance you want. No one can able to stop you and no one can able to cut your wings.

Divyanshu Singh

Divyanshu singh is a writer and poet from the land of great Rajasthan (bharatpur).
His writing skills is lit.
He also worked in 5+ books as a co-author
He writes only for himself and his loved ones...
follow him on Instagram @bharatpur_shayar

1.हमारी मुलाक़ात तो कई बार हुई।
फरक बस इतना सा है,
उसे याद नहीं और मैं भुला नहीं।

2. उनका दर्द दर्द हमार क्या मजाक था।
अगर उन्होंने इश्क़ किया,
तो क्या हमने फरेव किया था।

3.मेरी मोहब्बत को वो फरेव समझ बैठी।
मेने तो उसकी रूह से इश्क़ किया था,
मगर वो जिशमानी समझ बैठी।।

4. ऐ जानम तेरी उल्फत ने बेवफा बना दिया हमें,
तेरे फितूर मे हयात से बेवफाई कर ली हमने।

5. तुझसे दूर जाने का मेरा मेरा दिल नहीं करता,
तेरे पास रहने का मेरा मन नहीं करता।
तुझसे नफरत करने का मेरा जी नहीं करता,
और तुझसे प्यार कर सकू मुझे ऐसा कोई मंजर नहीं दिखता।।

6.ऐसा भी क्या गुन्हा किया हमने,
जो दलील बिना फैसला सुना दिया तुमने।
एक बार पूछ कर तो देखती,
खुद कि सच्चाई भी तो तुम्हे पता चलती।।

Devendra Fagna

Devendra gurjar is a writer and poet from the land of great Rajasthan (karauli).
His writing skills is lit.
He worked as Co-author in more than 7 books.
His love has no story that's why he start writing.....
#D4VE
follow him on Instagram @dev_fagna1 &
@kuch.adhuri_batein

1. इश्क़ तो हमने किया था, उन्होंने तो नफरत की थी....
देखकर भी उनकी नफरत को,
हमने दिल लगाने की कोशिश की थी...

2. उसके शब्दों के वार कुछ इस प्रकार हुए,
दिल को चीरते हुए तीर सीने के पार हुए...
छलनी कर गई वो हमारे दिल को,
ना फिर कभी हम दिल लगाने को तैयार हुए...

3. मुझको पत्थर कर दिया,
इस दिल को तोड़कर...
अच्छे खासे थे तेरे बिन,
क्यों रख दिया हमें झंजोड़कर....

4. तुझसे इश्क की ख्वाइश रखना तो पहले ही छोड़ दिया...
अब तो उन पुरानी यादों को जलाते हैं...
अपनी इस जिंदगी में रोज एक नई आग सुलगाते हैं...

5 . इश्क में दिल पे वार कई बार हुए,
एक बार भी जुड़ा नही दिल...
और हम बार-बार तुड़वाने को तैयार हुए...

6. इश्क ना करके कोई गुनाह कर दिया...
आपने तो हमें सारे जमाने में बदनाम कर दिया...

Payal Kamdi

Payal Kamdi resides in Maharashtra.
Penning her thoughts by penname Nityashree.
A girl with passion in writing mess with the heart and mind.The picking of ink and fell down of paper which cames along shadow. She belives writing helps to concrete thoughts and manifest faster. Really glad to be part of this anthology.

Never trust a mirror
Cause it always lies.
My day begin with you
I stare through your eye lenses
Looking into your eye
It touches my soul
Every moment I fell in you
I found myself.
Little things have changed
You made me little lesser
Uff! You made half cup of tea
Later on forget to put sugar
Did you really forget ?

In my dreamy you entered
Unknowingly locked your individual
In companion I myself too.
You broke my dreamy world
I shaatered everywhere
Unfortunately came near to you.
All the thoughts string in love
Slowly slowly broken in pieces.
The unloving chapter brings
How ? Why ? What ? I don't know
I just know it enters in my love
My existence, my nightmare gets smashed
In my true world.

Rahul Barman

He is a man with lots of imagination. The way he thinks is quite different as his thoughts are practical and harsh to take in. He started writing with quotes then came up with writing poems and also started to write stories. He believes, "One who is not emotional, can not be a writer."

You can follow him on insta @_chippy_20_

Like Nothing Happened

"Dreams were taking his last breath, who knew it? Everything changed like nothing happened."
Everything was fine until the day I got drunk. It was the blockhead me, who called my brother after getting drunk. I was absolutely out of mind, what actually was going on but am pretty blessed to have a brother like him, managed everything like nothing happened. Suddenly my eyes shuttered down and the shutter opened directly the next day.

I knew that people used to do a lot of shit after they get drunk, though I had to believe it this time. Almost said everything which I never dreamt of sharing, the love story of Maeve and Sid. Every part of my body and soul believes to be of Sid. David was very frank with me in every aspect but didn't thought of him to be that strict to me in this case. He took me to a riverside, I was so happy for being around my brother in such a beautiful place. All of a sudden, he asked me, "Is there anything you think I should be known of." But I said with all my guts together, "No, brother, I don't think there is something you should be aware of and not aware." Then the real story started when he asked me about Sid. I was shocked, "How could he come to know about all this stuff", but unluckily he knew everything. He asked me to break up with him and that sentence uttered from the lips of David was poison to me. David said that he was a kind a girl addict but it was me who didn't believe David and asked for a last chance. I move mountain to make my brother believe that he would change himself, but woefully I failed.

With all my guts I texted him, "Hii babe! After a lot of thoughts, I decided to end it up here. Never ever thought like it would end up like this but it's me, ending it up." "Okay.. so bye...." is what he said.

A year later, I was..........

Rupanjana Das

She's an artist and writer hailing from Kolkata who dreams to write her solo book. However she's also from psychology background and also a tattoo beginner. Currently residing in Calcutta, West Bengal, the 17 year old teen weaves up her own stories.

You can follow her on insta @blurrd_nights

A Dead Winter Evening

On the evening of a dead winter,
I lay on the bench like a fallen leaf
Disintegrated from my own soul,
As the cold wind turned bitter.
The house was still in view,
the broken pieces of our future showed
A never ending trail of the memories.
But he's no more in my life, I knew.
My aching heart was pleading to return
And the ring brought a second thought
But I knew I couldn't undo the scenes
I've been cheated on and tortured a lot.
I turned my back from the negativity.
Started walking amidst the nothingness.
I stopped to realise that doing good
for myself made the pain a little less.

Sakshi Soni

Writer for a reason, a lot left to cherish and win. Driver of my own thought, will lead sky someday. My words are louder than my thoughts

Barish ka time tha Waise toh wo mere saath job pr hi tha pr wo Kuch jyada hi special tha baaki ke couligs ke comparison main usko deekhte hi Aachakaise behatar feel hone lagta chalu mil jata ussdin baarishhorahi thi or mujhe ride pr jane ka mannn hai bola ki ride pr chalte hai Aachanak se baarish or tezhogyi usne Kaha no nahi jate hai kabhi or chalange pr zid ke aage Kaha sunnewalithi main main usko jabardasti leke gyikaafi Dar takbaarish main bightehue aab mujhe thandi lagane lagi thi Maine usko pyaarse pakad liya peeche se or poucha ki Koi problem toh nahi usne kuch nahi Kaha aise hi raste main saath chalte hue bike pr traffic main usne pyaarse mere haath ko pakada or mujhe uss time aisa feel hua no kaash ye haath kabhi na chute ....

Kuch time baad usne bike roka or main jab bike se utriham dono Waise toh poore bighe hi the usne mujhe Aachanak se gale laga liya or usne Kaha ki main uske liye bohot special ho Waise mera dream tha ki mujhe mera lifepartner aise hi harish main propose kre or so aapna poora bhi ho raha hai Sunke kaafi Aacha lagraha tha ye sab pr dar bhi tha kahi mera sapna tòot naa jaye .....

Uske baad usne mujhe mere sir pr kiss kiya or apne baho main bhar liya Waise gale toh aaksar lagatatha wo Mujhe jab usse kuch tension hoti thi toh pr aaj ki baat kuch or thi usne mujhe mere lips pr halka sa kiss kiya or main usstime poori uski ho chuki thi mujhe kaafi Aacha lagraha tha wo paljo uske saath beetarahi thi main mujhe aisa lag raha tha ki bas yahi chahie zindagi main or kuch nahi phir kuch time baad hum waha se nikle aate time merechahare pr alag hi kushi thi jaise Maine jo mujhe paanaho wo paaliya hai Waisikushi....

Aise time bitta gya mentally physically hai tarah se uski madadkrneke baad has tarah se uskosupport krneke baad aaj usse aisa lagta hai ki main Kisi Or ko like krti ho pr main usko Kitni baar samjha chuki ho ki wahi meri zindagi hai sab kuch hai Waise usne mujhe chod diya 1.5yrs ki relation ko usne 1 galatfahami ki wajahse tod diya pr mujhe aajbhi uska intazar hai or agar wo aaya toh uski saari galtiya maaf hai Kyuki aaphi apni zindagi se Kabtak koi narazho sakta hai.......

Saurav Kumar

A man with massive brain and distinguished caliber. Smart in all field. Aiming high to achieve everything. A hobbyist by mature. Keen to learn everything.

Fuggy Fuzzy Story Of "S"

Things will always fall into place
In good time
I will wait
Until you are not mine

We will be together
In good time
Some tears, some grudges
It's all fine

I'll be there to make you strong
In good time
Whenever we will meet
ll have a Royal dine

Come back to me, back to stay
In good time
I'll stand for you
From morning to evening nine

This life will not be a maze
In good time
I know, life is tough
Twist, turns, lulls, delays in line

Hope this wait gets over
In good time
This smiled face will proudly say
You are totally mine

Supriti Vishwakarma

Words her emotions and writing her power.
A girl full of passion and imaginative thoughts with a touch
of creativity and flexibility.
Lover of books and music, currently pursuing B. Tech.
Approachable at @supriti_vishwakarma on Instagram

I came back here
and felt it again
the pain of betrayal
of me being more loyal

It hurts hard always
the loosing of our faith
locked between much feelings
fighting against all the hate

I fell down again today
the flashback was like yesterday
all spirits got shattered
all convictions got crumbled

Today, I ask myself
can I do this again
To all the broken promises
can I make you again

Shradha Gindlani

Hailing from a small town with big dreams, Shradha Gindlani is a teacher in profession and a writer in her inner callings.She has compiled an anthology ' Bitter Truth ' and has been a co-author in a number of anthologies. With a vision of a community aiming at serving ones in need and upholding those who are part of it, she makes it to be humble and kind hearted.

I May Not Flower From You

While I stood as farm mannequin in a barren land
Your rained upon me
The hard times ploughed me again and again
You sowed me softly
When I had to push myself against the dusty criticism
You nourished me with calmness
While I had to bear the natural harshness from natures
You urged me to follow my nature's call

Abruptly though

I may not flower from your love
But you are my love.

Ashiya Khatun

Pursuing BPT
State - Assam
Hobies- dairy writing and singing.
Ambition- To become a good doctor and to serve positivity
and love.She loves to travel.
Turning my dreams into vision and vision into reality.
Currently saying yes to new adventure.

Every Togetherness Has A Bond

It was peak or class 12th, when I prepared myself for dope of love. The excellence sheet of our love depicts 30 sept as first day Of meet, but we didn't see each other. Longing for some beautiful months we met on 9th nov 2017. It was ocassion of birthday, we started talking and cherishing each other's innocence. I remember, he added first proposal and I pumped NO. Yes, my ethics didn't allow me. Perhaps I was coward to some sort. Anyway, I recycled my brain and added YES on second proposal.

So, my love started on 19th Dec 2017. We enjoyed 3 beautiful months. Yes, just 3 beautiful months. Then after I was chocked, my heart was hammered and shattered. We broke up. All this happened due to some cunning third eye. But flow of feelings could not make us apart. I has feelings, A relevant feeling for a relevant soul.

What's next, we rejoined this iconic bond on 20th may. We had some beautiful trip. We share all shortcomings and success together. It's been 3.5 years. And I am sure we will March till eternity.

Ankita Nahar

Ankita Nahar, physically she live in Rajasthan but heartly live in everywhere.

She is too much passionate about writing.

She have always found comfort in words, and thats what attracts everyone.Writing is her therapy, she write what she feels and experiences in her life. You can take a look at her writings on Instagram @naharankita1

I did not sleep all night
 I Just thinking about you
 To anger me like this
 Was needless or justified

 I was shouting on you
 I knew this behaviour was not good
 For you and for me also

My trust was broken
I can not trust you
Even just because of you
I can not trust anyone
My heart was broken
So i did not sleep whole night
It is a very big deal for me
Even big deal for my family also

FINALLY I DECIDE
I came to end with the relationship
FINALLY I DECIDE
I Don't want to talk
FINALLY I DECIDE
I Don't want to meet
FINALLY I DECIDE
Nothing to do now
Now all is over
You are finshed our relationship
By your side
I knew I am late
But It is my turn now

Insha Nayyar

She is pursuing graduation in commerce. A girl of her will. Transparent soul with heavy thoughts. Open heart and diversified brain. She loves connecting people.

You can follow her on insta @Inshanayyar0

Girls

Were ransomed
Not with perishable thing
But with blood of Christ (GOD)
Fearfully and wonderfully made
More valuable than rubies

A excellent craftsmanship of Creator GOD
Who loves her infinitely
Lets hold the truth GOD has
And plan something beautiful for her life

Girls and women
Feather, standing in same line
Have the right
To earn equal pay
To do whatever she wants with her body
To wear whatever she wish to

But the society
Crip and creep
Judge them abruptly
Pushes concept of post gender Society
Culture prizes women
On the basis of sexual attractiveness

Let's change the mindset
It's not an empowerment
But a myth buster
A step today
Will shower result tomorrow

A step today
Will shower result tomorrow

Rahul Kumar

He is brother by bond, A strong soul with vivid potent. Once decided, he can achieve anything. Currently he is doctor in making.

You can follow him on insta @Rahul6788kumar

Her love was uncertain
So is death
We were in love
Experiencing a harmonal surge

We started at peak age of Eighteen
With pact to help each other
My love, outsoaring her love
Sings a loftier song

To portray our relationship
I would consult
All rainbows and butterflies
I would bring
All stars and moon together

Our love was combination of
Compassion and passion
A strong Bonding
With an iconic relation

She drowning in cooings of my love
'Z expecting a long lasting love
Sitting alone in spares
Assuming arial view of us

But
On one night
I realise, I am in game with her
So she ran and hid
Game of hide and seek
'M still searching
'M still searching

Saddam Saikh

Caretaker of soul and understanding force. He will stand at any point, no matter what. King of own thought.

You can follow him on insta @Saddam_saikh8969224966

I am the king of night
Bowing down, as it's demise
'M seduced by my own wrath
I am not lewd, it's my attitude

I behave, as if I am elite
I tailor my own technique
For sure it's unique
I'm not lewd, it's my attitude

What I do is always right
With innerself, I always fight
Darkest of night are my best friend
I'm not lewd, it's my attitude

I am not like other social blight
I'll kill you , stay quiet
Stay away from my sight
I am the king of my night

Flairs and Glairs, a platform by a student for the students. We are esteemed youth struggling to carve out our path for our future and we follow a basic mindset Since everyone is not born with all-round skills. Joining hands with people who are born to execute it with perfection is the best way to evolve. Self-Evolution is the need of the hour but, evolving as a community is what we strive for. The initiative as kickstarted by, Founder- Mr. Shubham Shah with the motive to utilize the skillset and talent of writing has now a team of 10+ people who are actively participating into newer forms of learning and discovering talents among youngsters. We Provide platform and services like Publishing opportunities, Open mics, Workshops, Hands-on training. Operating with Brand Name of Flairs and Glairs (Publication House), we offer the chance of elevating a passionate writer to an esteemed author With Brand name Teekhe Zasbaaat. We bring to you an opportunity to get accustomed with the Public Speaking and Presenting of Thoughts along with regular challenges to brush up your inking spirit. The newest initiative to extend our services we introduced in a new writing Platform- The Glittering Fables and Ink Over Tears.

We Choose to Fly Like A Falcon than to be

a Leg Pulling Crab.

To Know More: Infoline – 7781900870
Mail Us At-
flairsandglairs@gmail.com / info@flairsandglairs.in
Or Visit is at
www.flairsandglairs.com / www.flairsandglairs.in
Social Handles- @flairsandglairs @teekhezasbaaat